mojo
mayhem

CARTOON NETWORK ®

by E.S. Mooney
Based on
"THE POWERPUFF GIRLS,"
as created by Craig McCracken

SCHOLASTIC INC.

New York   Toronto   London   Auckland   Sydney
Mexico City   New Delhi   Hong Kong   Buenos Aires

ISBN 0-439-33212-5

Designed by Peter Koblish

Illustrated by Barry Goldberg

12 11 10 9 8 7 6 5 4 3 2 1   2 3 4 5 6/0

Printed in the U.S.A.
First Scholastic printing, February 2002

SUGAR . . .

SPICE . . .

AND EVERYTHING NICE . . .

These were the ingredients chosen to

create the perfect little girl.

But Professor Utonium accidentally

added an extra ingredient to

the concoction —

CHEMICAL X!

And thus, The Powerpuff Girls were born!

Using their ultra superpowers,

BLOSSOM,

BUBBLES,

and BUTTERCUP

have dedicated their lives to fighting crime

and the forces of evil!

Chapter 1

The city of Townsville! A thriving, tranquil town . . . a virtuous, vibrant village . . . a merry, mild municipality . . .

But what's this? Why, the Gangreen Gang is stealing candy from the back of that truck!

A candy delivery truck was parked in an alley behind a candy store. The Gangreen Gang — Ace, Little Arturo, Big Billy, Snake, and Grubber — were huddled around the truck.

"Get ready to stuff your pockets!" Ace,

the leader, said. He forced open the back of the truck.

Big Billy broke into a huge grin. "Mmm! Free candy!"

Grubber just began to drool.

The Gang started taking boxes of candy out of the truck.

But who's this swooping down on the scene? Why, of course! It's The Powerpuff Girls, Townsville's own little superheroes!

Blossom, Bubbles, and Buttercup zoomed in and landed in front of the Gangreen Gang.

"You're in violation of Townsville ordinance number 3702," Blossom announced. "Unauthorized removal of privately owned edible material from a vehicle of transport and delivery."

"Plus, stealing candy isn't nice!" Bubbles added.

"So now we're going to have to beat you up," Buttercup explained.

In a flash of pink, blue, and green, the Girls had attacked the Gangreen Gang. Blossom grabbed Ace and Snake and knocked their heads together. *CRACK!* Bubbles swung Little Arturo above her head and let him fly. *WHEE!* And Buttercup socked Big Billy in the stomach, sending him staggering backward so he landed on top of Grubber. *THUD!*

The Girls returned the candy to the truck and sealed the door closed. Then they flew off toward home.

All in a day's work for the world's sweetest superheroes! And so, once again, the day is saved, thanks to — hey, where is that evil snarling coming from?

Why, it's Mojo Jojo, watching the whole

thing on one of his closed-circuit Townsville TVs.

Mojo Jojo, evil genius monkey and enemy of The Powerpuff Girls, thumped his white-gloved fist on the table in front of him.

"Curse you, Powerpuff Girls! You always spoil my favorite reality crime shows! You continually stop the villains of Townsville when I, Mojo Jojo, am trying to enjoy watching their evil deeds!"

That's right, Mojo! The bad guys of Townsville don't have a chance against The Powerpuff Girls!

All right, then, where was I? Oh, right . . .

. . . The city of Townsville! A handsome, happy hamlet . . . a congenial, caring community . . . a booming, blissful burg . . .

Wait a minute! What's happening now?

Who is that stealing coins from that vending machine? Why, it's Femme Fatale!

Woman-power supervillain Femme Fatale crouched in front of a *Townsville Times* newspaper vending machine. As usual, she was after Susan B. Anthony and Sacajawea dollar coins.

"The only money worth stealing," she declared. "That is, until they finally start making the Amelia Earhart dollar, the Betsy Ross quarter, and the Gloria Steinem penny!"

But wait! Here come The Powerpuff Girls!

Blossom, Bubbles, and Buttercup zoomed in.

"You're in violation of Townsville ordinance number 1701! That's unauthorized removal of currency from a
mechanical commerce device," Blossom
announced.

"Plus, stealing money isn't nice!"
Bubbles added.

"So now we're going to have to beat you
up," Buttercup explained.

In a flurry of fighting, the Girls sent
Femme Fatale packing.

*And so, once again, the day is saved,
thanks to The Powerpuff Girls!*

*But wait, where is that evil-sounding
stamping coming from?*

Once again, Mojo Jojo was watching the
whole thing on one of his TV screens.

Mojo stamped his white-booted feet
and let out a yell. "Aaaaah! What is the

matter with the villains of Townsville? Can't the criminals of this city do anything right? Can't the lawbreakers of our land complete a simple, unlawful task?"

I guess not, Mojo. It looks like the bad guys are no match for The Powerpuff Girls.

Now, ahem, once again . . .

. . . The city of Townsville! A marvelous, meritorious metropolis . . . a successful, serene settlement . . . a peaceful, pleasant pueblo . . .

Hold on! Look at those disgusting creeps coughing on people! It's the Amoeba Boys!

The Amoeba Boys, the lowest criminal life-forms in Townsville, were standing in the middle of a busy street. Bossman, Tiny, and Slim were coughing on people as they walked by.

But wait, here come The Powerpuff Girls!

"You're not even breaking any Townsville ordinances," Blossom said with disgust. "This isn't even a crime!"

"It's just very yucky!" Bubbles added.

"We're not even going to bother to beat you up," Buttercup explained.

The Amoeba Boys, looking disappointed, slinked off down the street.

And so, once again, the day is . . . well, maybe not exactly saved . . . Let's just say The Powerpuff Girls showed up once more to protect the citizens of Townsville!

But wait, where are the sounds of that evil tantrum-throwing coming from?

This time, Mojo Jojo was lying on the floor, kicking, pounding, and screaming.

"The Townsville villains are pathetic fools! They are incompetent idiots! They are an embarrassment to evil everywhere! They are not good at what they do!"

Mojo couldn't take it anymore. He fumed. He shook his fists in the air in frustration. Then, he had an idea.

"The criminals in this town need to be taught a lesson! And I, Mojo Jojo, shall be the one to teach it to them!"

Oh, no! What could that mean? Just what sinister scheme does Mojo have in mind?

Mojo Jojo stood on a platform in front of a large classroom. Seated in front of him at rows of desks were all of Townsville's villains.

Femme Fatale was in the front row, a small scowl on her face and a GIRLS RULE! notebook on the desk in front of her.

Behind her, squirming in their seats, were Bossman, Tiny, and Slim, the Amoeba Boys.

Also in the front row was Princess Morbucks, Townsville's own spoiled-rotten bad girl. She held a diamond-studded pencil case in her hand.

Next to Princess was Fuzzy Lumpkins, the half-witted hillbilly. Fuzzy had a great big lunch pail at his feet. He was busy twiddling his thumbs. Next to Fuzzy was Him, Townsville's most horrible villain. He didn't have any school supplies at all, but he was stroking a stuffed mouse. He looked a little bored.

The Gangreen Gang — Ace, Little Ar turo, Big Billy, Snake, and Grubber — were scattered across the classroom. They were all slouched in their seats. Little Arturo was combing his hair. Grubber was blowing spitballs. Ace sat in the front row.

Behind him was a big purple monster. Nobody recognized him. He wore a sticker that read HELLO, MY NAME IS GARY.

"Welcome to the Townsville Villain Academy," Mojo began. "At this school, I, Professor Mojo Jojo, will teach you, the students, how to be better villains. I, Professor Mojo Jojo, will train you, the pupils, to destroy properly. I, Professor Mojo Jojo, will instruct you, the trainees, to demolish correctly. I, Professor Mojo Jojo —"

"We get the idea, Mojo," Him interrupted.

"That's *Professor* Mojo to you!" Mojo said.

"Okay, sure thing, *ProMo*," Him sneered.

Fuzzy Lumpkins raised his hand. "Is it gonna be eatin' time soon, Teacher? I'm a-feelin' perdy hungry, and my possum stew's a-startin' to get cold."

Princess raised her hand. "I didn't bring any lunch. My daddy gave me money instead." She waved a fistful of bills in the air.

"Aha! Another example of men using money to control everything!" Femme Fatale stood up. "Speaking of which, I demand to know why we have a male teacher instead of a female teacher!"

"Be quiet, all of you!" Mojo yelled. "Stop talking! Be silent!"

Everybody stopped talking. The only sound in the room was the scratching of a pencil in a notebook. Gary, the large purple monster, was taking detailed notes.

"Now," Mojo began again. "I, Professor Mojo Jojo, am the teacher. That means that I, Professor Mojo Jojo, will do the talking. Which means that you, the students, will not be talking." Mojo took a deep breath. "Now, let us start with the fundamentals. The three R's of being a villain — Ruining, Robbing, and Ransacking. Your first assignment is Ruining. I, Professor Mojo Jojo, want each of you to choose something here in Townsville. And then I, Professor Mojo Jojo, want you to ruin it. Class dismissed."

Oh, no! Twelve of Townsville's worst villains (plus one out-of-town monster) all set on ruining Townsville?

The next day!

The students filed into their seats at the Townsville Villain Academy. Mojo stood in his place at the head of the classroom. A big, expectant smile was spread across his face.

"Good morning, class!" he greeted them. "We will now have the student presentations of the homework. You will each stand and describe for the class what you ruined, and how you ruined it."

Fuzzy Lumpkins's hand shot up. "Oh, Teacher! Teacher! I couldn't do ma homework."

Mojo scowled. "Why not?"

"I tricd!" Fuzzy said. "I was a-gonna ruin the Townsville Zoo, see? But just as soon as I started bendin' back those bars on the cages, The Powerpuff Girls showed up an' stopped me!"

"Duh, the same thing happened to us, right, Ace?" Big Billy called out from the back row.

"We wanted to trash the Townsville Supermarket," Ace explained. "But those pain-in-the-neck Powerpuff Girls showed up and ruined our plan."

Everyone in the classroom started talking at once. It turned out that just about all of the students had been stopped from doing their homework by The Powerpuff Girls. (All except Him, who hadn't felt like doing it, and Gary, who said he did his homework but his dog ate it.)

Mojo jumped up and down. He was furious. "You call yourselves villains?" he screamed. "You call yourselves criminals? You call yourselves bad guys?"

Femme Fatale stood up indignantly. "I object to the label bad *guy*!" she said. "The correct term is evil *person*."

"Sit down!" Mojo Jojo yelled. "You are all an embarrassment to evility! Well, I, Professor Mojo Jojo, will show you how it is done."

"Oh, is that so, ProMo?" Him mocked.

"Yes!" Mojo bellowed. "Now I, Professor Mojo Jojo, supergenius evil villain monkey and founder of the Townsville

Villain Academy, will show you, the fool-ish students, how to get things done."

The class was silent, watching him.

"Tomorrow we will go on a field trip," Mojo announced. "Tomorrow night we will go to rob the Townsville Jewelry Store. And we will not let any pesky Powerpuff Girls stop us!"

Chapter 3

The next night!

Mojo led his class through the dark streets of Townsville. They were headed toward the Townsville Jewel Emporium.

The students all wore special night-vision goggles Mojo had given them. Each of them carried a special Mojo-Jojo-style laser blaster.

"Everybody stay with your buddy!" Mojo announced to the class.

The class trooped along after him.

When they got to the window of the jewelry store, Mojo stopped and put up his hand.

"Now, class, what do we do next?" Mojo asked his students. "Who knows?"

"Bust through the glass?" Fuzzy suggested.

"Ask Daddy to buy all the jewels in the store so we don't have to do anything?" Princess said.

"Graffiti up the window?" Ace suggested.

"Go home, take a nice hot bath, and

forget all this?" Him remarked with a yawn.

"No!" Mojo said with exasperation. "You're all wrong! We use the special slicing lasers on our blasters to cut a hole in the window. Come on, everybody. Set your laser dial to 'slice.'"

The students all set their laser dials to "slice." All except Him, who set his to "refreshing cool mist," which he thought was more pleasant.

Mojo showed the class how to use their lasers to cut through the glass. Soon there was a hole big enough for them all to climb through.

Once they were inside, Mojo led them through several rooms of jewelry.

"Hoo-eey! Lookey at all this-here sparkly stuff!" Fuzzy said.

"I threw nicer things than these in the trash yesterday," Princess scoffed.

"Who cares about all this girly stuff?" Ace commented.

"I resent that," Femme Fatale announced. "And I'd like to add that I'm against jewelry on principle."

Mojo led them to a huge metal vault. "Now, set your blasters to 'decode,'" he instructed. He showed the class how to use their lasers to un-scramble the elec-tronic lock on the vault.

The door to the vault swung open. In-side was a velvet-covered pedestal. On top of the pedestal was a huge, sparkling diamond.

Everybody stared at the diamond. Everyone except Him, who had gotten bored. He'd decided to go home and rent a movie.

The Amoeba Boys headed toward the diamond eagerly.

"Stop!" Mojo bellowed. "You cannot just go up to that diamond! You cannot simply approach it!"

The Amoeba Boys froze in their tracks.

"There is a complicated laser-alarm system surrounding this diamond," Mojo explained. "If you walk through the lasers, an alarm will sound. Bells will ring. Buzzers will sound. People will know that you are stealing the diamond. And then those pesky Powerpuff Girls will come! Now, watch closely."

Mojo reached into his pocket and pulled out a collapsible fishing rod. He expanded the rod to its full length and attached the hook to the back of his belt. Then he handed the rod to Fuzzy Lumpkins. "Now, simply cast me inside the laser alarm and lower me down to the diamond," he told Fuzzy.

"Yee-haw!" Fuzzy cried. "This-here's just like fishin' for catfish down by the creek!"

Fuzzy cast the line and began to lower Mojo down to the enormous diamond.

"So you see, class," Mojo said to the watching students, "this is how it is done. This is how a professional villain gets things accomplished. This is how a master criminal —"

But Mojo was interrupted by a loud crash. Plaster and bricks flew every where. Blossom, Bubbles, and Buttercup burst in through the wall of the store.

"Hold it right there, Mojo!" Blossom said. "Don't move!"

Fuzzy's jaw dropped open in surprise. He let go of the reel, and Mojo dropped to the ground with a thud.

"I said don't move!" Blossom yelled at Mojo.

Bubbles looked around, her blue eyes wide. "Boy, there sure are a lot of people here. Is this some kind of a party?"

"Yeah, a beat-'em-up party!" Buttercup announced.

Gary, the purple monster, immediately excused himself and fled.

Blossom, Bubbles, and Buttercup attacked

the rest of the villains. Blossom zoomed over to
Femme Fatale and fo-
cused her eye beams on
her. The force of the eye
beams propelled Femme
Fatale high into the air.

Then Blossom turned off her eye beams and
let Femme Fatale drop. She landed on a dis-
play of jewelry.

Bubbles took on Princess Morbucks,
grabbing her by the crown. She slammed
Princess back and forth over her head,
smashing her down first on one side and
then the other.

Meanwhile, Buttercup started in on the
Gangreen Gang. She hit Ace with a one-
two punch, then floored Snake with a series of high-powered kicks. Soon her

sisters joined her.
Blossom used her ice
breath to freeze Big
Billy into a giant
statue. Then Bub-
bles zoomed after
Little Arturo and
Grubber, picking
them up and tossing them into the giant
vault.

Terrified by what was going on, Bossman, Tiny, and Slim immediately slunk
away.

Next Blossom turned toward Fuzzy
Lumpkins. Fuzzy was still holding the
fishing rod and watching them, his mouth
hanging open. Mojo was still hooked to
the end of the line. Blossom grabbed the
fishing rod from him and began to swing

it around over her head. Mojo began a wild orbit around the room.

Every time Mojo passed by Bubbles, she kicked him in the backside. When he flew by Buttercup, she socked him in the nose. Finally, Blossom let the line wind down, swirling it around Fuzzy. He and Mojo ended up tied to each other, hopelessly tangled together in fishing line.

"Well, our work here is done, Girls," Blossom said to her sisters.

Buttercup looked around the room. Bad guys were strewn everywhere. "Yeah, I guess there's nobody left to fight," she agreed reluctantly.

"Let's go home and have some milk and cookies," Bubbles suggested brightly.

Nice work, Girls! Guess your little field trip didn't work out so well after all, Mojo!

chapter 4

The next day!

The students of the Townsville Villain Academy limped into the classroom. Many of them were bruised from the fight with The Powerpuff Girls the night before. Several wore bandages.

Mojo stood at the front of the room, an eye-patch on one eye and a crutch in his hand. "I, Professor Mojo Jojo, am very disappointed in you, the students!" Mojo yelled. "The field trip last night was a disaster!"

"Actually, my movie wasn't so great, either," Him commented. "I mean, it was worth renting, I guess, but I wouldn't pay to see it in a theater."

"Because of you students, the trip was a failure!" Mojo went on. "A catastrophe! It was very bad! You must try harder and pay attention. Also, you must pay attention and try harder!"

A scratching sound came from the back of the room as Gary scribbled in his notebook.

"I, Professor Mojo Jojo, am giving you another assignment," Mojo announced. "This time, I, Professor Mojo Jojo, want you each to steal something." He glared at his students. "I, Professor Mojo Jojo, want you to select something — anything — and then I, Professor Mojo Jojo, want you to steal it! And don't let those Power-puff Girls get in your way!"

The following afternoon!

Fuzzy Lumpkins walked toward the Townsville Art Museum. He was whistling to himself. His lunch pail dangled from a loop on his pants. His favorite shotgun was slung over his shoulder.

"I'm a-gonna steal some art an' perdy

up ma property," Fuzzy said to himself. "Teacher's gonna be real prouda me."

Fuzzy waved howdy to the people at the museum entrance and walked inside.

In the first room, Fuzzy stopped in front of a painting of a woman. The woman was dressed in a long velvet gown. Her hair was piled on top of her head. A small, fluffy white dog sat on her lap.

"Too fancy," Fuzzy decided.

In the next room, Fuzzy stopped in front of a sculpture. The sculpture was made up of metal triangles attached together.

"Too confusing," Fuzzy said, moving on.

In the next room, Fuzzy stopped in front

of another painting. It was of a giant can of baked beans.

Fuzzy studied the painting. "Well," he said, "I knows what I likes. And I likes beans."

Fuzzy reached for the painting and pulled it off the wall. Immediately an alarm sounded, and two guards came running into the room.

"Stop, thief!" one of the guards yelled.

Fuzzy whipped around. "Thief? Where? Oh, y'all mean me!" He chuckled.

The guards drew their guns.

Fuzzy put down the painting. Then he took out his enormous shotgun and began blasting shots around the room.

Terrified, the two guards dropped their weapons. Fuzzy picked up the two men and hung them from the hook where the painting had been. Then he tucked the painting under one arm.

"Now, don't y'all go makin' any more trouble, hear?" Fuzzy said to the guards. "This-here's ma homework, see?"

Suddenly, there was a crash. Glass flew everywhere as The Powerpuff Girls smashed through the window.

"Aw, shucks!" Fuzzy said when he saw the Girls. "Not y'all again!"

"That's right, Fuzzy," Buttercup said. "It's us, The Powerpuff Girls. And now we're going to beat you up!"

"But y'all are gonna ruin ma homework!" Fuzzy objected.

Buttercup was ready to wallop Fuzzy, but Blossom stopped her. "Hold on a minute," Blossom said. "Did you say *homework*?"

"Why sure!" Fuzzy said. "I gots ta steal somethin'. It's fer the Townsville Villain Academy, ma school."

"The Townsville Villain Academy?" Bubbles asked. "I've never heard of that!"

"It's a real nice school," Fuzzy said. "We learns the three R's — Rippin', Roarin', and . . . aw, what are those three R's agin? Teacher told us, but I plum fergot!"

"Who exactly is this teacher, Fuzzy?" Blossom asked, her eyes narrowing.

"Why, I don't know if he ever done told us his name. I just calls him Teacher," Fuzzy said with a shrug.

"Come on, enough yapping," Buttercup complained. "Let's boat him up now."

"Wait a minute," Blossom said, thinking. "Does this teacher by any chance have green skin and a purple-and-white helmet?"

Fuzzy broke into a grin. "Sure, that's him!"

Bubbles gasped. "Why, that sounds like —"

"I know," Blossom whispered. "Just play along, okay? I have an idea." She turned back to Fuzzy. "That's a very nice artwork you have there, Fuzzy."

Fuzzy grinned again. "I'm a-gonna use it to perdy up ma property."

"You know, there's another picture in this room that's even better," Blossom said.

Fuzzy looked around. "There is? Where?"

"Right over there," Blossom said, indicating a red and white exit sign near the door. "Don't you think that one's really special, Girls?"

Bubbles giggled. "I guess so."

"Whatever," Buttercup said. "Can't we beat him up now?"

"In fact, that one's so special, they hung it up really high, where no one can reach it," Blossom continued.

"I bets I cain reach it," Fuzzy said. He dropped the bean painting and loped over to the the wall. Then he reached up and ripped down the exit sign.

"That one's really something," Blossom said. "That's the one I would steal, if I were going to steal one."

Bubbles gasped. "Blossom! You would never steal!"

Blossom winked at her. "But it sure is a pretty one!"

"Ya think?" Fuzzy eyed the exit sign. "Yer right, I reckon. This-here will really perdy up ma property. Teacher's gonna be real prouda me! So long, ever'body!" He headed out the door with the sign.

Bubbles giggled again. "I can't believe he just stole the exit sign instead of the painting! That was funny!"

Buttercup scowled. "I can't believe we didn't fight him at all! That was dumb!"

"No, it wasn't," Blossom said firmly. "It was all part of my plan."

"What plan?" Butter-cup grumbled. "The Wimp Plan?"

"No," Blossom shot back. "The plan to get Mojo. Didn't you hear Fuzzy? Mojo's behind all this. He's running some sort of Villain Academy. If we'd beaten up Fuzzy, then he would have gone back and told Mojo. And then Mojo might figure out that we're onto him. Anyway, listen . . . here's the rest of my plan. . . ."

chapter 5

Professor M. Jojo
Principal, Townsville Villain Academy
Townsville, USA

Dear Professor Jojo,

  As you may be aware, the National Association of Evil Education will be holding our annual Evilympics in your area soon. The Association would like to take this opportunity to invite the Townsville Villain Academy to send a team to participate in this year's Evilympics.

The Evilympics are an excellent opportunity for the students at your school to test themselves against representatives of the finest evil educational institutions in the world.

We look forward to your participation.

Sincerely,
National Association of Evil Education

Mojo read the letter and jumped up and down with excitement.

"The Evilympics! This is great! This is terrific!" he cried happily. "If we can bring home some medals, all my hard work will have paid off! Those ungrateful students! The long hours of planning lessons and ordering supplies! Those ungrateful students! The after-school tutoring sessions! All of it will have been worthwhile!"

Mojo let out a long sigh, dreaming of a trophy case filled with medals from the Evilympics.

"Finally," he said, "a chance for Townsville's villains to prove themselves!"

Chapter 6

The next day!

Mojo Jojo stood in front of his students.

"I, Professor Mojo Jojo, have a very important announcement," he said. "Our team uniforms for the Evilympics have arrived."

He reached into a large box in front of him and pulled out a uniform. The uniform was a purple-and-green jumpsuit with the letters T.V.A. on it.

"In these uniforms, you can feel proud

of yourselves on the playing field," Mojo announced. "Now, come on, everybody! Together now! Go, Townsville!"

"Go, Townsville!" the students called out.

"Excuse me, I'd like to order one with fur trim," Princess Morbucks announced.

The next day!
Mojo Jojo stood in front of his students.

"I, Professor Mojo Jojo, have a very important announcement," he said. "Our team banners have arrived."

He reached into a large box in front of

him and pulled out a banner The banner was green with purple lettering that read TOWNSVILLE VILLAIN ACADEMY.

"These banners will proclaim our school pride. Okay, come on, everybody," Mojo said. "Together now! Go, Townsville!"

"Go, Townsville!" the students called out.

"Hoo-ey! I reckon this is gonna be some hoedown!" Fuzzy said with a grin.

The next day!
Mojo Jojo stood in front of his students.

"I, Professor Mojo Jojo, have a very important announcement," he said. "Our team mascot has arrived."

He opened the door beside him. A giant yellow banana walked in. The banana was

wearing a large purple-and-white turban and a purple cape.

"Now, this is a mascot to be proud of! Come on, everybody," Mojo said. "Together now! Go, Townsville!"

"Go, Townsville!" the students called out.

"Nice cape," Him remarked. "Does it come in red?"

The next day!
Mojo Jojo stood in front of his students.

"I, Professor Mojo Jojo, have a very important announcement," he said. "Our team song is ready."

He handed out copies of the song.

"Everybody sing together now," Mojo instructed.

"Let's hear it for T.V.A.!
Let's hear it for T.V.A.!
We're feeling full of evil,
We're gonna cause upheaval!
We're gonna do some bad today!
Let's hear it for T.V.A.!
Let's hear it for T.V.A.!
We will not be forgotten,
'Cause we're the fighting rotten!
And dirty is how we play!"

Mojo wiped a tear from his eye as he finished the song. "Once again, everybody," he said. "Together now! Go, Townsville!"

"Go, Townsville!" the students called out.

"That song would sound much cooler with some electric guitar," Ace commented.

The next day!

Mojo Jojo stood in front of his students.

"I, Professor Mojo Jojo, have a very important announcement," he said. "We now have a team cheerleader."

He opened the door beside him. Gary, the giant purple monster, stepped out. He was wearing a purple pleated skirt and holding green-and-purple pom-poms in his hands.

"Gary brought a note from home excusing him from the Evilympics," Mojo explained. "But he will be cheering the rest of you on."

Gary waved the pom-poms in the air, jumped up, and landed in a split.

"Everybody," Mojo said. "Together now! Go, Townsville!"

"Go, Townsville!" the students called out.

"I'm against cheerleaders on principle," Femme Fatale objected.

chapter 7

The day of the Evilympics has arrived! All of the Townsville Villain Academy's rotten-to-the-core student body is gathered together in Townsville Central Park.

"All right, team," Mojo said. "This is our big chance, our opportunity, our moment of glory!"

His team stood in front of him in a line. (All except Him, who had decided to stay home and reorganize his kitchen cabinets.) They were dressed in their purple-

and-green T.V.A. uniforms. Gary was wearing his cheerleader's suit and waving his pom-poms.

"I, Professor Mojo Jojo, believe that we can win this!" Mojo said. "I have faith that we can triumph! I am certain that we can be victorious!"

"Excuse me?" Princess Morbucks said. She was wearing a special gold crown with a big amethyst on it. "Where are the other teams?"

Mojo looked around in surprise. He had been so excited about his pep talk to the team that he hadn't noticed that they were the only ones there.

"Oh, er —" Mojo began.

But he was interrupted by a swooshing sound from high above him. Three objects cut across the sky at a high speed, leaving trails of pink, blue, and green be hind them.

"Oh, no!" Mojo yelled. "It's the —"

"That's right, Mojo," Blossom said, landing on the grass in front of him. "It's The Powerpuff Girls!"

"Hoo-ey!" Fuzzy Lumpkins said. "Do y'all have your own evil academy, too?"

"Of course not!" Bubbles said indignantly, landing on the grass beside her sister. "We *fight* evil!"

Buttercup swooped down. "And today that means we're gonna fight *you*!"

"B-b-but what about the Evilympics?" Mojo stammered.

Blossom grinned. "We'll show you some Evilympics, all right! Come on, Girls!" Blossom zoomed forward and grabbed Ace. "Our first event is the pole vault!" she announced.

Blossom zoomed
forward, using
Ace as a pole to
vault high into the
sky. As Blossom
sailed up into the
air, her sisters lined
up the rest of the
Gang as hurdles.
They leaped over Big Billy, Grubber, Snake,
and Little Arturo, then crushed them into
the ground with their feet.

"And now for some weight lifting!" Buttercup announced.

She heaved Fuzzy Lumpkins over her
head like a barbell. She held him up there
for a moment and then smashed him to
the ground.

Bubbles zoomed toward Femme Fatale.

"How about a javelin toss?" she said. She grabbed the supervillain and threw her hard across the field like a spear.

Buttercup swooped toward the Amoeba Boys. "Discus throw!" she yelled. She grabbed the slimy bad guys and hurled them toward Bubbles.

"Hurdles!" Bubbles yelled. She leaped over each of the Amoeba Boys just before they smashed into a nearby wall.

Blossom flew over to Princess Morbucks. "How about some gymnastics?" she said.

Blossom picked up Princess and launched into a series of punches that put Princess Morbucks through an amazing sequence of flips and spins through the air.

Bubbles and Buttercup watched and applauded.

"And we'll finish with the *floor* routine," Blossom said, hurling Princess to the ground.

Bubbles and Buttercup each raised a scorecard above their heads, like judges. Their scorecards both read "0."

"And now for the last of today's events," Buttercup said. "Evilympic-style soccer!"

She zoomed over to Mojo, picked him up, and sent him flying across the field.

Blossom intercepted, dribbling Mojo back down the field with her feet.

Blossom passed to Bubbles, who kicked Mojo through the air, landing him in a garbage can.

"Goal!" Bubbles yelled.

"Yay!" the three Girls cheered.

Just then, the big purple monster walked up to them. He handed Blossom a note.

Please excuse Gary from participating in fighting.
Thank you,
Gary's mother

Gary turned and walked away down the field.

Buttercup turned to her sisters. "Who's he?"

"Beats me." Blossom shrugged.

"He seemed kind of nice," Bubbles commented.

"Anyway, the important thing is that Mojo Jojo's Villain Academy is history!" Blossom announced.

"That's right!" Buttercup agreed.

"Looks like school's out for good!" Bubbles giggled.

Aw, shucks, Girls! That's one lesson plan for success. And so, once again, the day is saved by The Powerpuff Girls!

Cartoon **CARTOON** FRIDAYS f

FRIDAYS 8-11pm et/pt

CARTOON NETWORK

CartoonNetwork.com